Richard Scarry's
GIANT
Storybook Treasury

12 BOOKS IN ONE

Richard Scarry's
GIANT
Storybook Treasury

J.B. COMMUNICATIONS, INC.

Published 2004 by J.B. Communications Inc., New York, NY

Previously published by J.B. Communications Inc. as
Richard Scarry's Busy Day Storybooks and
Richard Scarry's Little First Learners

ISBN 0 8056 5009 1

Pre-press: 69 – Studio Reklamy, Olsztyn, Poland, EU

Printed and bound in India

CONTENTS

Richard Scarry's
Mother Cat's Busy Day

It is early in the morning, before the sun comes up. A light goes on in the Cat family house.

"Mommy, I'm hungry!" says Little Sally Cat.

For Mother Cat, it's the start of another busy day!

In the kitchen, Mother Cat
prepares breakfast for the Cat family.

While everyone eats,
she makes sandwiches
for Huckle's and
Lowly's lunchboxes.

It is time for the Cat family to be on its way.
Mother Cat quickly loads the washing machine.

Father Cat goes out to the car through the back door. *BANG!*
Sally and Huckle follow him. *BANG! BANG!*
Then Lowly. *BANG!*

"Really," says Mother Cat, "I must get that banging door repaired."

The Cat family drives away.

First, Mother Cat drops off Huckle and Lowly at the school bus stop.

"Goodbye, Mom!" waves Huckle.
"Goodbye, Mrs. Cat!" waves Lowly.
"Have fun at school today!" calls Mrs. Cat.

Then Mother Cat brings Sally
to the kindergarten.

Mrs. Murphy, the kindergarten teacher, awaits them.
"Welcome, Sally!" she says.
Mother Cat gives Sally a kiss, and then drives Father Cat
to the train station. He has an important business trip to
Workville today.

Now Mother Cat has some errands to run. By chance, she sees Mr. Fixit in his repair truck.

"Good morning, Mrs. Cat," says Mr. Fixit. "Can you please come over to our house and fix a banging back door?" Mother Cat asks Mr. Fixit. "Sure thing, Mrs. Cat!" Mr. Fixit replies. "There's nothing Mr. Fixit can't fix!"

While Mother Cat goes food shopping at the supermarket,
Mr. Fixit inspects the Cat family back door.
"Hmmm," he says.

After shopping, Mother Cat takes a moment to rest at Mr. Raccoon's coffee shop.

"Good morning, Mrs. Cat," says Mr. Raccoon. "What can I bring you today?"
Mother Cat orders a cup of hot tea, and a bacon, lettuce, and tomato sandwich.

Meanwhile, Mr. Fixit starts to fix the Cat family back door. He removes the door with its hinges. SPROING!

He removes the doorframe from the wall.

He brings his biggest hammer from his repair truck.

Soon it is time for Mother Cat to pick up Sally from the kindergarten.

Sally has made a finger-painting for her mother. "Thank you, Sally," says Mother Cat, hugging her. "It's beautiful!"

Then she picks up Huckle and Lowly at the school bus stop. The boys have made Mother Cat a pencil-holder in class. "Thank you!" says Mother Cat. "This will be so useful by the telephone."

My!
Hasn't Mr. Fixit
been busy!
He pauses
to look at
his work.

Then he looks at the Cat family garage.
"Aha!" he says.

19

Mother Cat invites the children for sundaes at Bruno's ice-cream parlor. *Mmm!*

20

They have just enough time to finish before fetching Father Cat at the train station.

Father Cat has thoughtfully brought Mrs. Cat a bouquet of flowers.
"I had such a successful day!" he says.
Mother Cat takes the flowers and gives him a kiss.

"After so much driving around today, I think the Cat family car need some gas!" says Mother Cat.

Mother Cat drives into Scottie's filling station.

Look! Mr. Fixit is filling up his truck, too! "Did you have any luck with that banging door?" Mrs. Cat asks Mr. Fixit.

"Did I ever!" replies Mr. Fixit. "I promise you, that old door will never bang again."

My heavens, Mr. Fixit wasn't kidding! There surely is
nothing that Mr. Fixit can't fix for good. Why, he has even
built a new mailbox, swings for the children, and hung up
Mrs. Cat's laundry to dry!

"Wow, this is great, Mom!" says Huckle. "We must be the only family in Busytown with a drive-in kitchen!"

Richard Scarry's
The Firefighters' Busy Day

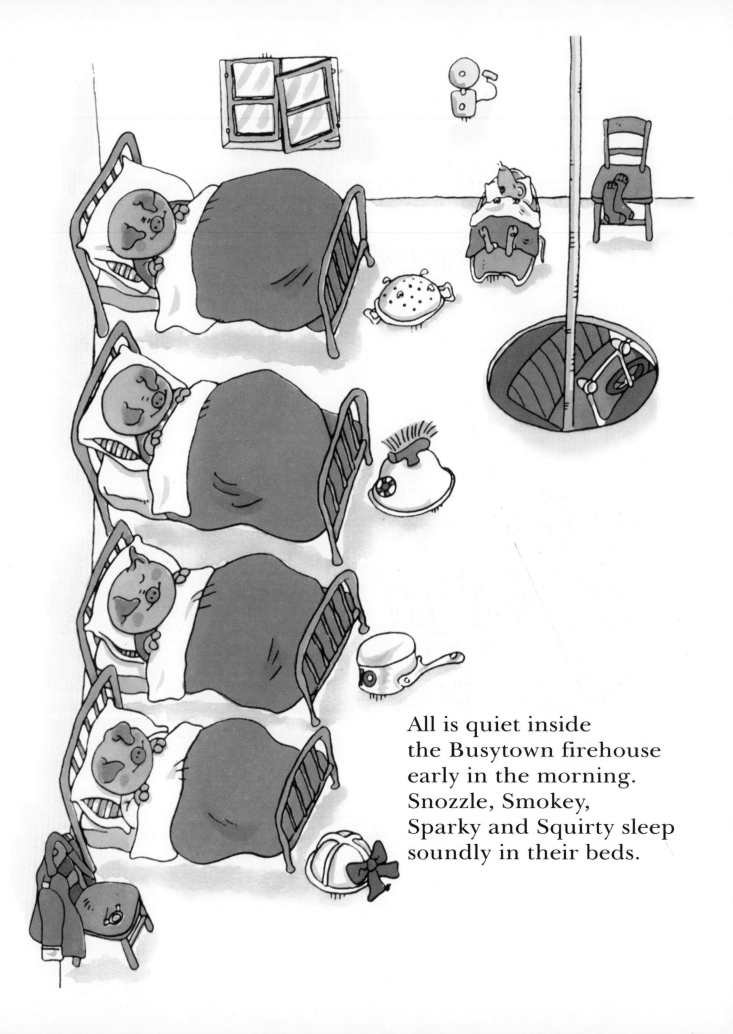

All is quiet inside
the Busytown firehouse
early in the morning.
Snozzle, Smokey,
Sparky and Squirty sleep
soundly in their beds.

"Drrinng!!!"
sounds the fire alarm.

The four firefighters jump from
their beds, put on their helmets,
and slide down the pole.
The fire engine waits downstairs.

Hurry,
firefighters!

The fire engine races
through the streets.
"Clang! Clang!" goes
the bell.
"Toot! Toot!" sounds
Sparky's horn.

Make way,
everybody!

32

They arrive at
Mr. Frumble's
house.
My! Look at all
that smoke!

Smokey, Sparky, Squirty and Snozzle burst through
the door, fire hose in hand.

Mr. Frumble is preparing burnt toast for breakfast.
Yum. Yum.

The firefighters drive back to the firehouse and sit down for breakfast.

Smokey prepares pancakes.

"Drrinng!!!" sounds the alarm again.

Sorry, firefighters! Breakfast will have to wait!

Off drive
the firefighters
to the rescue.

It's Mr. Frumble again.
His pickle car key
has fallen into
the gutter.
Smokey pulls it out
with a magnet.

The firefighters return
to the firehouse
to eat cold pancakes.

"Drrinnng!!!" sounds the alarm
once again.

The firetruck speeds once again
to the rescue.

Guess who
needs help?
Mr. Frumble
should learn
to drive more
carefully, don't
you think?

Smokey turns off the fire hydrant, and Mr. Frumble and his pickle car land softly on the street.

The firefighters return to the firehouse.

They decide to grill hot dogs.

"Drrinnng!!!" goes the alarm.

The firefighters race
to the rescue again.

Uh-oh. Now
Mr. Frumble
has lost his
hat in a tree.

Using a ladder, the firefighters fetch Mr. Frumble's hat and give it back to him.

"Drrinnng! Drrinnng!" goes the telephone on the firetruck. Smokey answers the phone. It's another alarm.

It's a FIRE!

The firefighters
hurry through the streets.

"Clang! Clang!"
"Toot! Toot!"
Watch out,
everybody!

Smoke billows out of a garage door. Squirty shoots
the water cannon. Sparky runs forward with the hose.
Hurry, firefighters!

"Whooosh!!!" With a spray of water,
the fire is out in an instant.

Good work, firefighters! Uh-oh. It was the firefighters' hot dogs.

I think you will have to find something else to eat.

"Drrinnng!!!"
sounds
the alarm.

Without wasting a minute,
the firefighters are off
to the next emergency.
Poor, hungry firefighters!

They arrive at Mr. Frumble's house again.
Mr. Frumble is having a bath.

I think your bathtub is full now, Mr. Frumble.

So that they can finally have a quiet moment
to eat, the firefighters invite Mr. Frumble to
have dinner with them at the firehouse.

Squirty stirs a big pot of firefighter stew.

Sparky brings out the bowls.

Everyone sits down at the table. Doesn't the stew smell good!

"Drrinnng!!!" goes the alarm.

The firefighters are off to the next rescue.
My, don't firefighters have a busy day!

Oh, bon appetit, Mr. Frumble!

Richard Scarry's
Rudolf Von Flugel's Busy Day

Rudolf von Flugel looks out of the window.
The sun is shining.
"What a perfect day to go flying!"
Rudolf says.

Rudolf washes, dresses and then has breakfast.
Guten Appetit, Rudolf!

Rudolf goes to his
balloon hangar and
chooses one for the day.

He brings
his balloon
outside onto
the airfield.

Huckle and Lowly
have come to watch
Rudolf take off.

"Ach! Your
shoelace is
not tied!"
Rudolf tells
Huckle.

Rudolf ties Huckle's shoelace.
Thank you, Rudolf.
Uh-Oh!
There goes Rudolf's balloon!

"I must bring
back my balloon!"
cries Rudolf.

57

He runs into his
airplane hangar.

He chooses an airplane and
drives out of the hangar.

58

BOOM!
BOOM!
You have
to open
the hangar
doors first,
Rudolf!

59

Rudolf opens the hangar
doors, and takes off in
another airplane.

He flies up.

He flies down.

He flies
upside-down.

Whoops!
Rudolf forgot
to fasten
his seatbelt.

Luckily,
he is
wearing
a parachute.

Now Rudolf has a balloon and an airplane to fetch.
Hurry, Rudolf!

63

Rudolf runs to
his helicopter hangar.

64

He chooses a helicopter
and flies out.

SMASH!

Please, Rudolf, next time, please leave
through the door... not the roof.

Up, up, up, Rudolf flies.
He flies into a cloud, and out again.

There's your
balloon,
Rudolf!

Be careful
not to get too close.
Watch out!

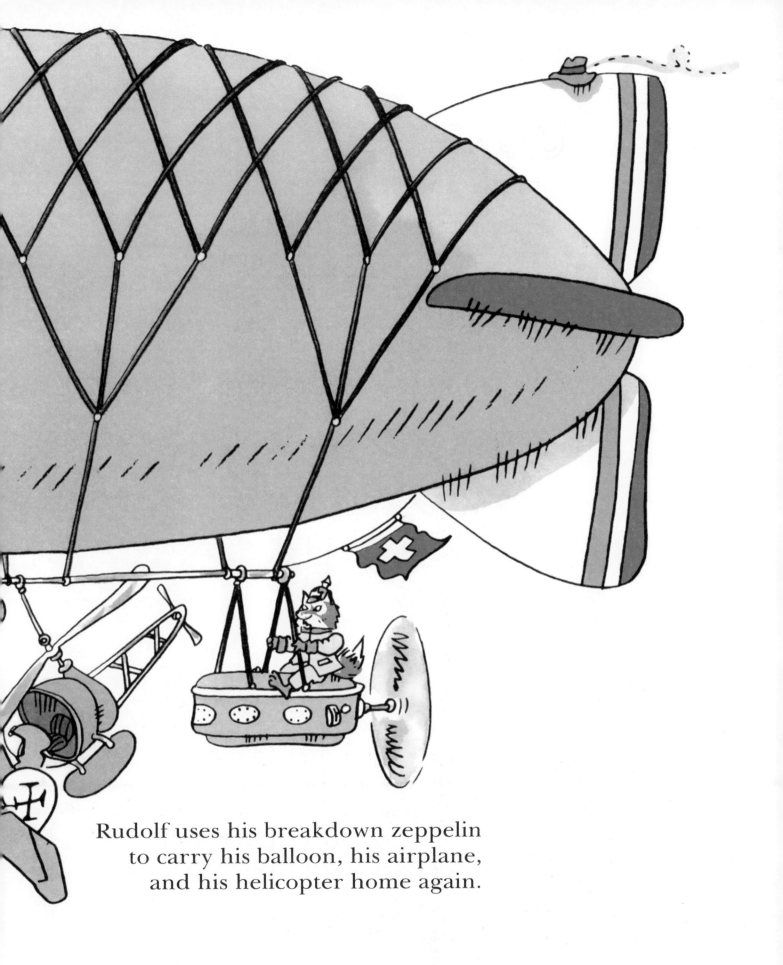

Rudolf uses his breakdown zeppelin
to carry his balloon, his airplane,
and his helicopter home again.

My, what a busy day it has been for Rudolf! Exhausted, Rudolf goes to bed. Schlaf gut!

Hmm. I wonder what Rudolf dreams of, don't you?

70

Richard Scarry's
Father Cat's Busy Day

It is early morning. Father Cat awakes as the sun comes up.

He looks out of the window. "What a perfect day to put the boat in the water!" he says.

He goes downstairs to the kitchen and prepares breakfast for the family.

He brings Mother Cat a cup of coffee in bed.

Father Cat runs outside to his sailboat,
parked beside the garage.

He pulls off the canvas cover, and tries to push the boat trailer into the driveway. But the trailer won't move. It has a flat tire. Ungh!

From the
garage,
Father Cat
gets an air
pump.
Just then, Mother Cat comes up on her bicycle, holding
a shopping list.
"I have to go the hairdresser," she says. "Could you
please do the food shopping for me this morning?"

Then Huckle arrives
with his bicycle,
Sally with her tricycle,
and Lowly with
his scooter.
Everyone needs air
in their tires!

Finally, Father Cat
can pump up the
trailer tire.

Then he pulls
the boat into
the driveway.

79

But it's time
to do the
shopping.

The boat trailer is blocking the
driveway!
Father Cat drives the Cat family
car around the boat, onto the lawn,
crushing a few bushes. Sorry, bushes!
He also knocks over the mailbox.

At the supermarket, Father Cat realizes he has forgotten Mother Cat's shopping list.
He asks the children to each choose three items from each shopping aisle. That should please Mother Cat.

After the supermarket,
the car needs some gas.
Father Cat drives into
Scotty's gas station.

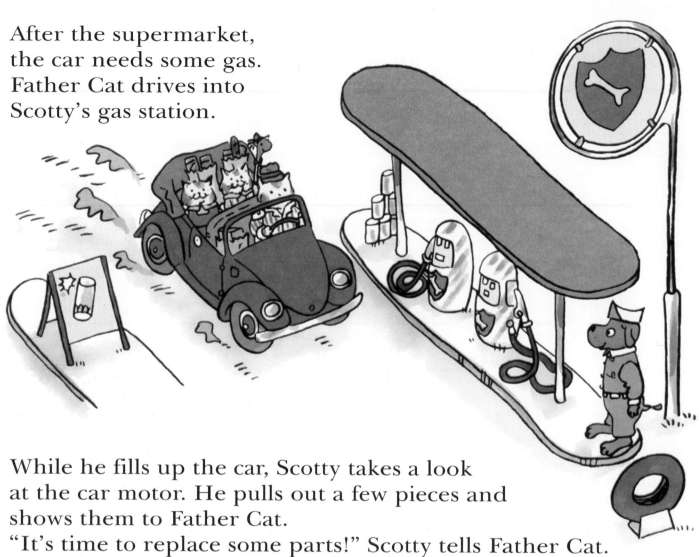

While he fills up the car, Scotty takes a look
at the car motor. He pulls out a few pieces and
shows them to Father Cat.
"It's time to replace some parts!" Scotty tells Father Cat.
"Don't worry, it won't take long."

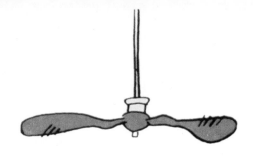

While Father Cat waits for his car to be repaired, he invites
the children across the street for milkshakes.

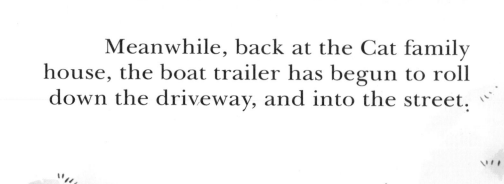

Meanwhile, back at the Cat family house, the boat trailer has begun to roll down the driveway, and into the street.

Oh, no!
Here comes
Mr. Frumble
in his
picklecar!

"Who would sail a boat into the
middle of the street!"
Mr. Frumble says.

CRASH!!!

Luckily, Mr. Fixit soon arrives on the scene.

With his crane, he removes Father Cat's boat out of harm's way. Then he tows away Mr. Frumble's broken picklecar.

"A good thing that you brought along a trailer, Mr. Frumble!" Mr. Fixit says.

Soon, the Cat family car is ready again.
It looks like the ice-cream somebody
chose at the supermarket has melted.

Now the car needs to go
through the car wash.

At last, they are ready to drive home.
Mother Cat must be wondering
what has happened to them!

But instead, Mother Cat is wondering what has happened to her poor bushes and the mailbox.

Father Cat looks with surprise at the driveway.

"What has happened to my boat?" he asks.

"I know I left the boat
in the driveway,"
Father Cat tells
Mother Cat. "It has
to be around here
somewhere!"

"Well,
before you begin to look,"
says Mother Cat, "perhaps you first
want to change out of your pyjamas!"

92

Richard Scarry's

Humperdink's
Busy Day

It is very early
in the morning.

All of Busytown
is still fast asleep.

"Drrinnng!" sounds the alarm clock next to Baker Humperdink's bed.

It is time for him to begin baking bread for hungry Busytowners!

Baker Humperdink rides off through the dark on his bicycle to the bakery.

Brushes drives by in his street sweeper. "Good morning, Humperdink!" calls Brushes. "Good morning, Brushes!" waves Humperdink. Humperdink stops at Able Baker Charlie's house.

Able Baker Charlie hops onto Humperdink's bicycle.

On their way to the bakery, they pass
the TV bug reporters.
They are out to report the morning's
news.

At the bakery, Humperdink and Able Baker Charlie first warm up the oven.

While the oven gets hot, Humperdink kneads bread dough made from flour, water, salt and yeast.

Able Baker Charlie makes different-shaped loaves of bread out of the bread dough.

Good work, Charlie!

When the loaves are ready, Humperdink and Able Baker Charlie put them in the oven.

Now they must wait for the loaves of bread to bake.

"What do you say we have a donut raffle today?" Humperdink asks Charlie.

Charlie agrees that it's a great idea. He prepares the raffle tickets while Humperdink makes the donuts.

Whoops! I think the bread is ready boys!

Humperdink and Able Baker Charlie run to the oven.

They take out the baked bread just in time.
Ummm! Doesn't it smell delicious?

While the bread cools, they put the donuts into the oven.

Once the loaves of bread have cooled, Humperdink places them in the bakery window.

Able Baker Charlie is going to make deliveries.
"Drive carefully, Charlie!" Humperdink says.

Charlie climbs onto his delivery bicycle and pedals away.

First he delivers long French baguettes to Louie's Restaurant.

"How are you today?" Louie asks Charlie. "Very well, thank you!" replies Able Baker Charlie.

Charlie then brings bread to Hank's market.

"Have a nice day, Charlie!" says Hank. "Thanks, Hank!" says Charlie pedaling away.

When Able Baker Charlie returns to the bakery, he sees the firefighters going inside.

"Have they come to buy some bread?" wonders Charlie.

NO! They have come to put out a burnt-donut fire! "Whooosh!" goes the firefighters' water hose.

When the fire is out, the firefighters leave the bakery.

"Don't forget to take a raffle ticket!" Humperdink says.

Humperdink starts to make a new batch of donuts.

Just then, Patience, the baby-sitter, arrives with little Sophie Humperdink.
"Could you please look after Sophie while I go to my dental appointment?" Patience asks Humperdink.
"No problem, Patience!" Humperdink says.

Both Humperdink and Able Baker Charlie are a little tired from getting up so early in the morning.

They decide to have a nap while the new donuts bake in the oven.

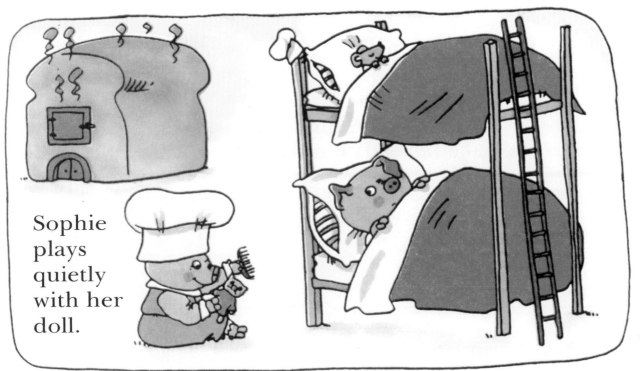

Sophie
plays
quietly
with her
doll.

Suddenly, Humperdink is awakened by a strange noise.

Oh no! It's the firefighters again!

Humperdink and Able Baker Charlie leap from their beds and take the baked donuts out of the oven just in time!

Good work, boys!

Now it is time for the raffle!
Humperdink reaches into his hat
to pull out the winning number.

He pulls out a ticket
and holds it up.

"The winning ticket..."
shouts Charlie,
"is number four!"

"That's OUR ticket!" says Smokey.
"We won the raffle!"

Baker Humperdink and Able Baker Charlie
bring out the big raffle prize.
The firefighters look very pleased.
They love to eat donuts.

The firefighters drive away with their prize.
"You know, Charlie," says Humperdink, "we haven't eaten a *thing* all day!"
They decide to have a good meal at Louie's Restaurant.

... a big bowl of breadcrumb soup!

Their favorite!

Richard Scarry's
Sergeant Murphy's Busy Day

Well before the sun is up, Sergeant Murphy's telephone
rings. "DRRINNNG!!!" Sergeant Murphy wakes up.
"Hallo?" he answers the telephone, "Sergeant Murphy here."
It is Deputy Flo calling from the police station.

"I have looked everywhere,
Sergeant Murphy," she says,
"but I can't find your
whistle! You can't work
today without it!"

"Don't worry, Flo," answers
Sergeant Murphy.
"My whistle is right here
beside me. Thanks
for calling!"

The Murphy family gets up for another busy day.

While Mrs. Patsy Murphy dresses little Bridget, Sergeant Murphy prepares breakfast.

Ummm! Don't those eggs and bacon smell good?

Soon it is time for Sergeant Murphy and Bridget to go.

Sergeant Murphy drives Bridget to the
kindergarten in his motorcycle's sidecar.

On the way, his motorcycle telephone begins to ring.
"DRRINNNG! DRRINNNG!"

It's Mrs. Murphy on
the line.

"Sarge, you left your
whistle behind this
morning, but don't
worry, I will leave it
at the police station."

Sergeant Murphy drops Bridget off at kindergarten. "Bye, Daddy!" calls Bridget, as she enters. "Goodbye, Bridget! Have fun!" calls Sergeant Murphy.

"DRRINNNG!" goes Sergeant Murphy's telephone. It's Mayor Fox calling. "Sergeant Murphy, there is a giant traffic jam outside. Busytown needs your help to clear it up."

"Yes sir, Mayor Fox!" replies Sergeant Murphy. "I'm on my way!"

But Sergeant Murphy wonders how he will direct traffic without his whistle.

Just then, he sees a band playing in the park. He stops and asks if he may borrow the cymbals.

With the cymbals tucked neatly in his sidecar, he speeds away.

My, what a traffic jam!
"Just stay calm, everybody!" Sergeant Murphy says.

"Clang!" Sergeant Murphy directs cars to the left.
"Clang!" He directs cars to the right.
The traffic jam is sorted out.

Good work!

125

Directing traffic makes Sergeant Murphy hungry.
He stops for a donut and hot chocolate at Humperdink's
bakery.

His telephone rings.
"DRRINNNG! DRRINNNG!" It's Deputy Flo, calling from
the police station.

"Mrs. Murphy has
brought your
whistle!" says Flo.

"Thank you, Flo!"
answers Sergeant
Murphy. "I'll be over
soon to fetch it."

But before he can
finish his donut, his
telephone rings again!

126

Why, it's little Sophie Pig. She is crying! While she was
shopping with her mother at the supermarket, she got lost.

"Don't worry, Sophie!" says Sergeant Murphy.
"I'm on my way!"
Before you can say "hot chocolate," he's off!

VRROOOM!

On the way, Sergeant Murphy's telephone rings again! It's Sophie's mother on the line. She, too, is crying! She can't find her daughter anywhere in the supermarket!

"Just stay calm!" Sergeant Murphy says. "I will find her for you."

At the supermarket, Sergeant Murphy finds Sophie and brings her to her mother. Thank goodness for Sergeant Murphy!

Sergeant Murphy looks at his watch. It's time to give a traffic-safety lesson at school!

"DRRINNNG!" sounds Sergeant Murphy's telephone.
It's Deputy Flo again.
"Sergeant Murphy, since you didn't come for your whistle,
I'm leaving it at Humperdink's bakery."
"Thank you, Flo," says Sergeant Murphy.

On his way to school, Sergeant Murphy wonders how he will instruct the children without his whistle. But he gets an idea and borrows Huckle's bicycle bell.

"Ring! Ring! Stop!" directs Sergeant Murphy. "Ring! Ring! GO!"

That's a pretty funny police whistle, Sergeant Murphy!

It is time for Sergeant Murphy to coach the school's soccer team.

Without his whistle to coach the team, Sergeant Murphy borrows a school band tuba.
Huckle kicks the soccer ball high in the sky, but no one sees it come down again.

"That ball went out of bounds!" says Sergeant Murphy.

He tries to blow the tuba, but no sound comes out. He blows harder...

"TOOOOT" sounds the tuba as the soccer ball flies out.

"That sure is the funniest coaching whistle I've ever seen!" laughs Huckle.

"But it works!" answers Sergeant Murphy, "TOOOOT!!!"

After soccer practice, Sergeant Murphy drives to pick up Bridget at the kindergarten.

"Hi Daddy!" she waves. "Have you had a busy day?"

"Oh, yes," replies Sergeant Murphy, "and my busy day is not yet finished!"
Sergeant Murphy drives with Bridget to Humperdink's bakery to pick up his whistle.

Able Baker Charlie
is there to greet them.

"I'm sorry, Sergeant
Murphy," Charlie says,
"Baker Humperdink just
left, and he took your
whistle with him!"
Poor Sergeant Murphy.

Just then, the telephone rings.

"It's for you!" says Charlie,
handing Sergeant Murphy the telephone.

It's Mrs. Murphy.

"Could you come
home soon, please,
Sarge? It's important!"
"Okay, Patsy!" he
replies. "We're on
our way home!"

What a surprise! Baker Humperdink, Sophie, Sophie's mother, Flo, and even Able Baker Charlie are there. Baker Humperdink hands Sergeant Murphy his whistle. "Thank you for having found our little Sophie today! I've baked you this whistle cake!" he says.

"My that's the funniest cake I've ever seen," says Sergeant Murphy, "but won't it taste good!"

0

Richard Scarry's
Miss Honey's Busy Day

The sun is up!
Miss Honey and Bruno wake from their sleep.

"Good morning, Bruno," says Miss Honey.
"Good morning, Miss Honey!" says Bruno, yawning.
"Did you sleep well?"

While Miss Honey
washes her face
and brushes her teeth
in the bathroom,
Bruno gets dressed.

Don't forget to wash,
too, Bruno!

Miss Honey and Bruno go to the kitchen.
Bruno sits down at the table.

"What would you like
for breakfast today, Bruno?"
Miss Honey asks.
"Chocolate ice cream, please!"
replies Bruno.

"But, Bruno," says Miss Honey, "you had chocolate ice cream for breakfast yesterday."

"Hmmm," thinks Bruno, "then today I'll have pistachio, okay?"

Bruno drives Miss Honey to school
in his ice cream truck.

At the school door,
she waves goodbye to him.
Soon school children arrive.

"Good morning, pupils!" Miss Honey says.
"Good morning, Miss Honey!" reply the children.

The children take their seats in the classroom,
and Miss Honey checks the attendance list.

"Hilda? Huckle? Lowly?... Vanderbuilt?" she asks.
Where is Vanderbuilt?"

Aa Bb Cc Dd Ee Ff Gg Hh Ii Jj Kk Ll Mm Nn

Suddenly Vanderbuilt appears in the door.
"Excuse me for being late, Miss Honey," Vanderbuilt says,
"Uncle Gronkle's car wouldn't start this morning!"

First, the class practices spelling.
"Who knows how to spell APPLE?"
asks Miss Honey.

Lowly spells, "A-P-P-L-E, apple!"
Good for you, Lowly!

Next, the class works with numbers.
Miss Honey asks Vanderbuilt to do
an addition.
Miss Honey is patient and helps
Vanderbuilt find the answer.

The class bell rings.
It's time for gym!

The pupils leave the classroom
to change into their sports uniforms
in the locker room.

The class plays a game of basketball with Mr. Tough. It's lots of fun!

Flossy Bunny shoots the ball into the net.

Good shot, Flossy!

After gym, it's time for lunch. The children join Miss Honey in the school cafeteria. There are many different things to choose from.

"Try to choose items from more than one food group," Miss Honey says. "That's the way to keep healthy!"

151

Then it's time for recess.
While everyone plays outside
in the school playground,
Miss Honey gives Bruno
a telephone call.

"What did you have
for lunch today, Bruno?"
Miss Honey asks.
"Ice cream!" replies Bruno.

"Bruno, you have to eat
something other than
just ice cream!" says
Miss Honey.
"Okay, Miss Honey, I
promise. Tomorrow I will
eat something different."

153

This afternoon, Miss Honey has a special treat for her class – a field trip to the Busytown Fire Station!

The class rides to the firehouse in the school bus.

Smokey greets them at the door.

"Wow!" says Huckle. "This is neat!"

The children learn all about the fire engine
and the firefighters' duties, and Snozzle
brings everyone refreshments.

As a surprise, the firefighters drive the class back
to school in the fire engine.

Aren't they lucky!
I think Miss
Honey enjoys the
return ride, too.

Back in the classroom, Miss Honey
asks the pupils to make a drawing of
the fire station to bring in to school
tomorrow.

The school bell rings, and Miss Honey's class heads home.
What a busy day it has been! Look! Here comes Bruno!
He has brought Miss Honey a rose.

"May I invite you
out to dinner
tonight, Miss
Honey?" he asks.
"Why, I'd be
delighted. Thank
you!" says Miss
Honey. "Where
shall we go?"

Why, of course, to Bruno's favorite,
the ice cream parlor!

Richard Scarry's
Mr. Gronkle's Busy Day

The sun has been up for hours, but it is still quiet at Mr. Gronkle's house. Mr. Gronkle likes to sleep late!

THUMP!

THUMP!

THUMP!

THUMP!

THUMP!

Strange sounds from upstairs
awake Mr. Gronkle.

THUMP!

THUMP!

THUMP!

"I can't get
any sleep!"
grumbles
Mr. Gronkle.

163

Mr. Gronkle gets out of bed and goes up to his visiting nephew's room.

"What are you doing, Vanderbuilt?" Mr. Gronkle demands. "Why don't you go play outside? I'm trying to sleep late."

Mr. Gronkle goes
back to bed.

Mr. Gronkle
gets out of bed.
He goes over
to the window.

"Can't you find a
quiet game to play,
Vanderbuilt?"
Mr. Gronkle shouts.
"Come inside and have
your brunch."

THAWCK!

"How about a game of chess, Uncle Gronkle?" Vanderbuilt suggests. "That doesn't make any noise!" "No!" replies Mr. Gronkle. "I'm busy reading my newspaper."

Mr. Gronkle gets dressed.

"Come along, Vanderbuilt," Mr. Gronkle says, "we're going outside."
"To fly this kite?" Vanderbuilt asks.

"No!" replies Mr. Gronkle. "It will probably land somewhere and I'll have to go fetch it. We're going for a drive."

Mr. Gronkle and Vanderbuilt drive out the gate.

"Are we going to get some ice cream?" ask Vanderbuilt. "No!" replies Mr. Gronkle. "I don't like ice cream. I like peace and quiet!"

"Is that YOU again, Vanderbuilt?"
Mr. Gronkle asks.

But Vanderbuilt
is quiet.

The sound is coming from the car.

Oh, no! Mr. Gronkle has a flat tire!

"What a fine day this is!" Mr. Gronkle grumbles.
"Come along, Vanderbuilt. We have to call for help."

Mr. Gronkle calls for help at a roadside telephone.
Mr. Fixit answers Mr. Gronkle's call.
"No trouble at all!" says Mr. Fixit. "I'll be right over!"

Mr. Gronkle and
Vanderbuilt sit on
a bench to wait for
Mr. Fixit.

"What a nuisance!" growls Mr. Gronkle.
"If I didn't have to take you out for a
drive, this never would have happened!"

"What do you mean, Uncle Gronkle?" Vanderbuilt says.

"You haven't done ANYTHING for me! You wouldn't let me play basketball in my room. You wouldn't let me play tennis outside. You wouldn't play chess with me, and we couldn't fly the kite!"

BONK!

Look out, Mr. Gronkle!
Huckle runs up to retrieve his soccer ball.

"I'm sorry, Mr. Gronkle," Huckle says. "It was an accident. Instead of sitting here, wouldn't you and Vanderbuilt like to play soccer with us? We could use some more players!"

"But I haven't played soccer since I was in school!" says Mr. Gronkle.
"Please! Please! Uncle Gronkle!" says Vanderbuilt. "It will be fun."

For someone who hasn't played in years,
Mr. Gronkle is a pretty good shot!

Mr. Gronkle scores a goal. Yay!

Mr. Gronkle can kick
the ball backwards.

Mr. Gronkle can kick the
ball sideways.

Mr. Gronkle scores another goal with a header!
And for the first time all day, Mr. Gronkle is SMILING!

"Your car is ready!"
says Mr. Fixit,
walking up.

"Why, thank you, Mr. Fixit," says Mr. Gronkle. "Won't you join us for a little soccer? You'd be surprised how much fun it can be to play!"

Richard Scarry's

Miss Honey's School Bus

Poor Spotty Leopard
wakes up with a bad
cold. "AAH-CHOO!"

He telephones Miss
Honey.
"I need to stay in bed
this morning," he says.
"Do you think you
could drive the school
bus for me?"

"I'd be very happy to, Spotty!" replies Miss Honey. "Get well soon!"

Bruno drives Miss Honey
to Spotty's school bus.
"Are you sure you can
drive it?" Bruno asks,
worried.

Miss Honey climbs into the driver's seat. She looks at all the gears and dials. "Hmm, this might not be so easy," she says. She puts the bus into reverse. BAM! She puts the bus into foward. BANG! Off she goes!

Meanwhile, at the bus stop, the school children are wondering where Spotty's school bus can be.

Miss Honey won't be happy if they arrive late for school!

Here comes the bus! Stand back everyone! Hey, that's not Spotty, it's Miss Honey who is driving the bus today! What a surprise!

Miss Honey turns to Billy Dog. "I don't know the bus route, Billy, so will you please tell me where to turn?" she asks.

"Sure thing!" replies Billy, proudly.

Off they go. Please drive slowly, Miss Honey, and mind that big bump up ahead!

BUMP! OW!

"Is everyone okay?" Miss Honey asks.

Everything is fine, except that now the bus has a flat tire!
Miss Honey changes the tire. GEE! What a job! WOW!
What a mess!

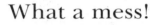

Soon the bus is on its way
again, but not for long. Now
it's out of gas!

Miss Honey walks to the nearest gas station to get some gasoline. Then she walks back, fills the gas tank, and continues on again.

"Turn here, Miss Honey!" shouts Billy.

Miss Honey turns.
But instead of
turning right,
Miss Honey turns left.

Uh-oh.

Whoops!

SPLASH!

Miss Honey and the school children climb onto the roof to wait for help.

"Boy, this has been the most exciting bus ride EVER!" says Huckle.

Luckily, Mr Fixit
arrives soon and pulls
the school bus out of
the water.

Mr. Fixit finally brings the children and the bus to school.

Spotty Leopard is waiting at the school house door.

"Thank you for driving the bus for me this morning, Miss Honey!" he says. "I'm feeling much better now."

"Yikes! My poor bus!"

Poor Spotty.

Now he's not feeling so well anymore. I think Miss Honey is a better school teacher than a school bus driver, don't you?

Richard Scarry's

Smokey's Fire Engine

Smokey is a
Busytown firefighter.

Smokey lives in the fire house
with the other firefighters.

Each firefighter has a different job
to do at the fire house to keep it neat and clean.

Sparky likes to
sweep the floors.

Snozzle likes to paint the walls.

Squeeky likes to do the laundry.

Squirty likes to cook
firefighter soup.

And Smokey always likes to keep the fire engine
shiny and clean!

Keeping the fire engine
clean is not easy.

Everyone else in the fire house
is busy cleaning, too!

First, Smokey takes
sponges and buckets of soapy water...

Hey, Sparky could you please sweep
the floor someplace else?
You are in my way.

Then, Smokey rinses off the soap
with a water hose...

Hey, Snozzle, please be careful not to drip paint on my truck. Thank you!

Finally, Smokey dries off the fire engine
with a cloth.

Excuse me, Squeeky, we're only drying the fire engine, not the laundry, too!

Now that Smokey's fire engine is shiny clean,
it's time for him to join the other firefighters for a bowl
of Squirty's firefighter soup!

Mmm! Bon appetit everyone!

Uh-oh, there goes the alarm!

The firefighters run to Smokey's shiny fire engine.
They are off to the rescue!

Maurice Moose's maple syrup truck has bumped into Molly Mole's molasses truck.

Nice going, Maurice! What a mess!

The firefighters hurry to clean up the spilled
maple syrup and molasses.

"Please be careful where you spray that water!" warns Smokey.

WOOSH!

Splash!

Poor Smokey!

Richard Scarry's
Cars and Trucks

DIFFERENT PEOPLE, DIFFERENT CARS

Mr. Paint Pig needs a truck with lots of space to carry paint and brushes.

mouse in a racing car

The Cat family likes to drive in an open four-seat convertible.

mouse in a pencil car

Sergeant Murphy drives
a bright red motorcycle.

Bananas Gorilla likes
his yellow
bananamobile.

Creamer Cat delivers fresh milk in his yellow van.

three bugs in a
green leaf car

flying pickles

dashing vintage roadster

Postman Pig picks up
mail in his mail van.

mailbox

great big tractor-trailer pickle truck

The Pig family drives in a station wagon.

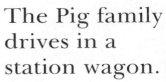

Lowly Worm always drives his apple car.

Harry Hyena on roller skates

AT THE GARAGE

Greasy George's garage is a busy place for cars to be repaired, washed, and filled-up with gasoline.

Greasy George

a car having a bath

happy mechanic

Gasoline is delivered to Greasy George's garage
in this tank truck.

delivery man

underground
gas tank

gas pump

Mother Cat's car gets a full tank of
gasoline, and a clean windshield.

CARS AND TRUCKS FOR BUSY HELPERS

siren

radio

The policeman needs a speedy car to get quickly where he is needed.

white ambulance to carry patients to the hospital

red fire trucks to race swiftly to a fire

tow trucks for repairmen ...

... and for
repair women

jingling bells

There is an ice-cream truck!

Here is a TV truck.

IN THE STREET

Here comes the garbage truck, picking up garbage.

garbage can

There goes the
street sweeper,
cleaning the street.

Here is an Army car.

There goes a scooter ...

... and there is
Mr. Frumble in
his pickle car.

Mind your hat,
Mr. Frumble!

BUSY MACHINES

Here is a bucket scoop, digging a ditch.

the surveyor's plan

a marker string

Earmuffs protect against the noise.

A compressor compresses air for the jackhammer.

a detour sign

The jackhammer digs up the pavement.

cone

240

Here is a crane
laying a pipe.

crane
operator

driver

Here are two
busy workers.

Hey! Stop chatting!

a jeep

241

steam-shovel
dumping rocks

tractor dumping
earth

bugdozer

an all-terrain
buggy

dump cart
carrying earth

242

dump truck not watching
where it dumps

bulldozer
pushing earth

Here is the school bus, carrying children to school.

WHICH CAR WOULD YOU LIKE TO DRIVE?

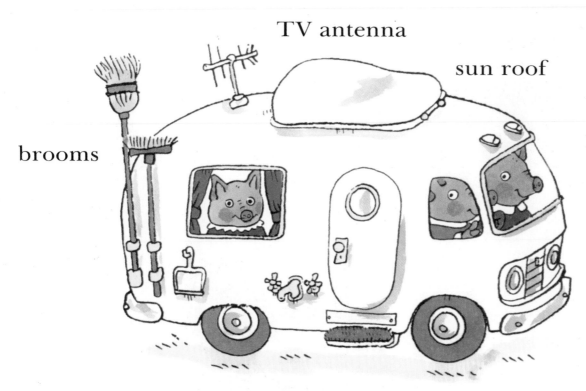

TV antenna

sun roof

brooms

The Pigs' camping car?

Mr. Fixit's hammer car?

mustard

Wilbur Rabbit's hot dog car?

Tommy's taxi?

Captain Salty's boat car?

A bug car?

Sprout Goat's tractor?

Or Dingo Dog's sports car?

Drive carefully!

Cars and

Trucks

Richard Scarry's

This is Me

WHAT A WONDERFUL PERSON I AM!

I can look.

I can walk.

I can run.

I can stand.

I can jump.

Sometimes I fall.

Ouch!

Be brave!

And sometimes I cry if I'm hurt.

LOOK WHAT I CAN DO

I can listen.

I can talk.

I can see.

I can smell.

I can touch.

I can eat. Yum!

And when I sleep,
I have nice dreams.

I can wash myself.

comb

I'M NO LONGER A BABY

I can comb myself.

I can take a bath by myself.

brush

soap

towel

water

I can brush my teeth.

toothpaste

I always put my things away neatly.
Mommy likes that.

Mommy has taught me to
sew on buttons ...

... and how to make my bed
all by myself.

THIS IS ME FROM THE FRONT

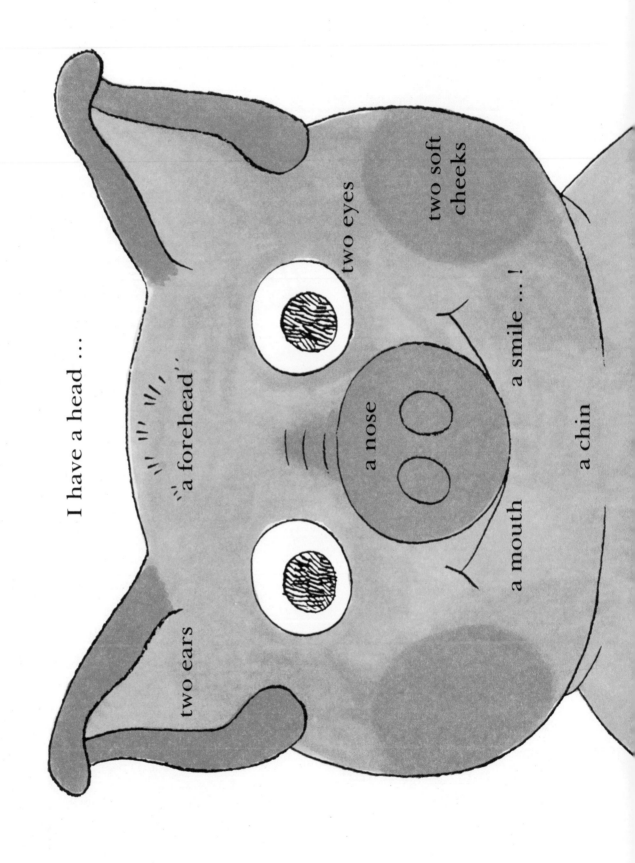

I have a head …

"a forehead"

two ears

two eyes

two soft cheeks

a nose

a smile …!

a mouth

a chin

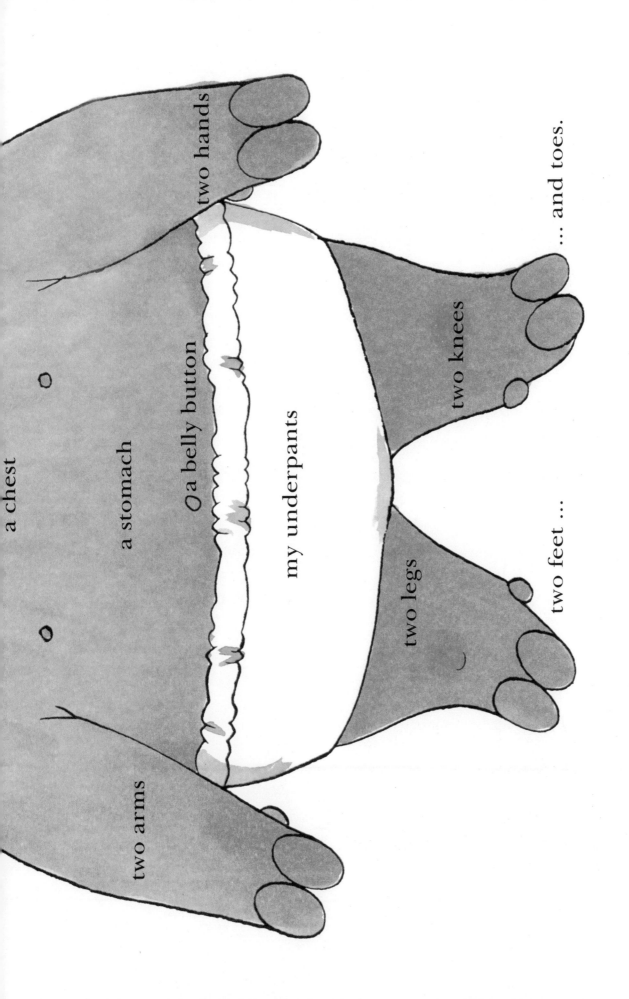

a chest

a stomach

a belly button

two hands

two arms

my underpants

two legs

two knees

two feet ...

... and toes.

259

THIS IS ME FROM BEHIND

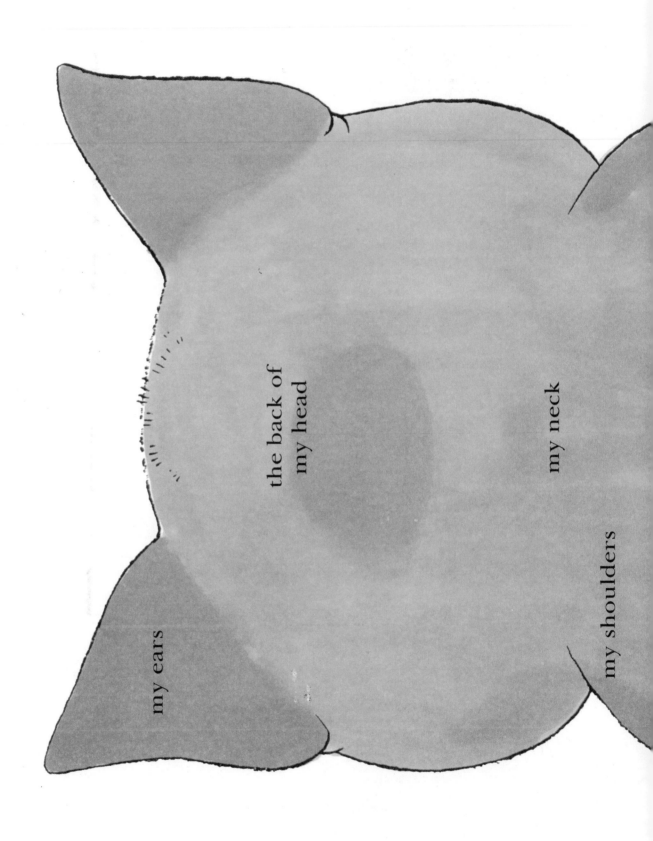

my ears

the back of
my head

my neck

my shoulders

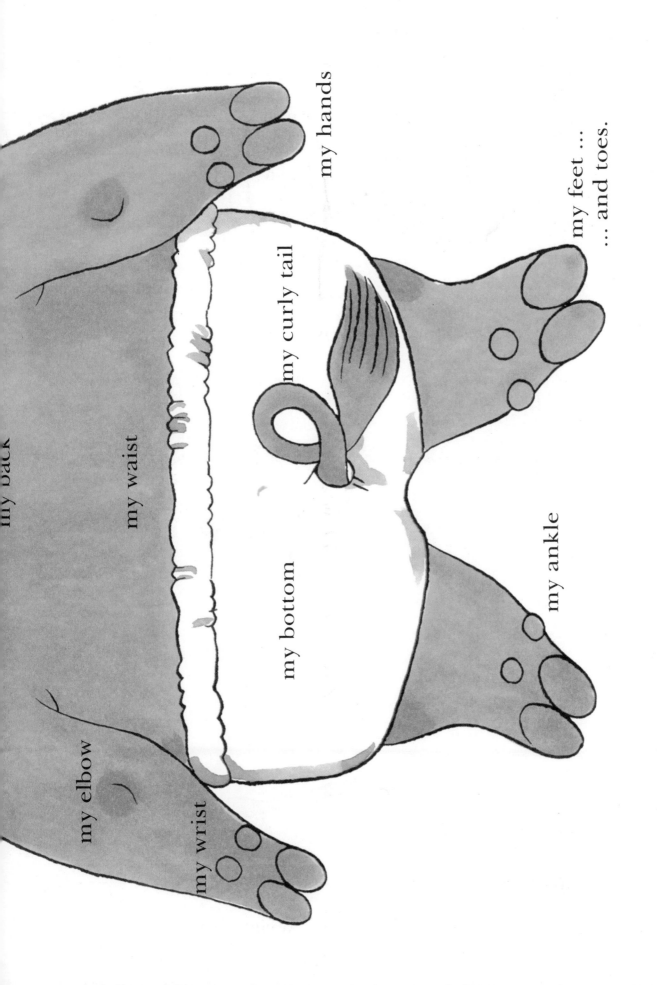

my back

my hands

my feet ...
... and toes.

my waist

my curly tail

my elbow

my ankle

my bottom

my wrist

LOOK AT ALL MY CLOTHES

shirt

blazer

overcoat

jacket

overalls

sweater

vest

undershirt

underpants

sneakers

belt

socks

wrist watch

blue jeans

dress

skirt

blouse

bonnet

purse

tights

handbag

hair comb

sunhat

headband

necklace

earrings

ring

I CAN DRESS MYSELF

closet

Hey! That's no way to put on your shorts!

suspenders

coat hanger

bathrobe

socks

cap

When I go to
a party, I get
dressed up.

bow

necktie

I bring flowers
as a gift.

slippers

sandals

pajamas

nightie

When I go to bed at night,
this is what I wear.

I DRESS DIFFERENTLY FOR ALL KINDS OF WEATHER

In winter, I dress for the cold.

earmuffs

mittens

wool hat

gloves

ski jacket

my sled

snowsuit

scarf

ice skates

When it rains. I dress to keep dry.

rainhat

umbrella

raincoat

boots

puddle

rubbers

In summer, at the beach, this is what I wear.

sunhat

sunglasses

swimsuit

This i

s Me